Green Light Readers

For the new reader who's ready to GO!

Amazing adventures await every young child who is eager to read.

Green Light Readers encourage children to explore, to imagine, and to grow through books. Created for beginning readers at two levels of skill, these lively illustrated stories have been carefully developed to reinforce reading basics taught at school and to make reading a fun and rewarding experience for children and grown-ups to share outside the classroom.

The grades and ages within each skill level are general guidelines only, and books included in both levels may feature any or all of the bulleted characteristics. When choosing a book for a new reader, remember that every child progresses at his or her own pace—be patient and supportive as the magic of reading takes hold.

❶ Buckle up!
Kindergarten–Grade 1: Developing reading skills, ages 5–7
- Short, simple stories • Fully illustrated • Familiar objects and situations
- Playful rhythms • Spoken language patterns of children
- Rhymes and repeated phrases • Strong link between text and art

2 Start the engine!
Grades 1–2: Reading with help, ages 6–8
- Longer stories, including nonfiction • Short chapters
- Generously illustrated • Less-familiar situations
- More fully developed characters • Creative language, including dialogue
- More subtle link between text and art

Green Light Readers incorporate characteristics detailed in the Reading Recovery model used by educators to assess the readability of texts through the end of first grade. Guidelines for reading levels for these readers have been developed with assistance from Mary Lou Meerson. An educational consultant, Ms. Meerson has been a classroom teacher, a language arts coordinator, an elementary school principal, and a university professor.

Published in collaboration with Harcourt School Publishers

A New Home

A New Hme

Tim Bowers

Green Light Readers
Harcourt, Inc.
San Diego   New York   London

www.harcourt.com

First Green Light Readers edition 2002
Green Light Readers is a trademark of Harcourt, Inc.,
registered in the United States of America and/or other jurisdictions.

Library of Congress Cataloging-in-Publication Data
Bowers, Tim.
A new home/Tim Bowers.
p. cm.
"Green Light Readers."
Summary: Matt the squirrel has a new home, but misses his old friends.
[1. Squirrels—Fiction. 2. Friendship—Fiction. 3. Moving, Household—Fiction.]
I. Title. II. Series.
PZ7.B6773Ne 2002
[E]—dc21   2001002370
ISBN 0-15-216564-9
ISBN 0-15-216570-3 (pb)

A C E G H F D B
A C E G H F D B (pb)

Matt has a new home.

Matt is sad.
Matt has no friends here.

This is Pam.
Pam has a new hat.

Oh no!
Pam lost the hat.

Matt has the hat.
The hat is here, Pam.

Matt has a new friend!

Pam has a new friend!

Meet the Author-Illustrator

Tim Bowers loves writing and illustrating books about friends. To come up with new story ideas, he thinks about his own friends from his hometown in Ohio. He always looks forward to meeting new friends as well!

Tim Bowers

Look for these other Green Light Readers
in affordably priced paperbacks and hardcovers!

Level 1/Kindergarten–Grade 1

And for older readers, look for
Level 2/Grades 1–2 Green Light Readers

Green Light Readers
For the new reader who's ready to GO!